St. María Faustina

A Treasury of Prayers from the
Diary of St. Maria Faustina Kowalska

Arranged and Introduced
by Colleen Free

Marian Press
Marians of the Immaculate Conception
Stockbridge, Massachusetts 01263

2000

Available from:
Marian Helpers Center
Stockbridge, MA 01263

Prayerline: 1-899-804-3823
Orderline: 1-800-462-7426
Website: www.marian.org

Editing and Proofreading:
Dave Came, Stephen LaChance, and
Mary Ellen McDonald

Typesetting: Mary Ellen McDonald

Cover Design: Paula Hegarty
Adapted from a scene in the video *Divine Mercy — No Escape;* St. Faustina is portrayed by actress Melanie Metcalf

For texts from the English Edition of the
Diary of Saint Faustina Kowalska

NIHIL OBSTAT:
George H. Pearce, SM
Former Archbishop of Suva, Fiji

IMPRIMATUR:
Joseph F. Maguire
Bishop of Springfield, MA
April 9, 1984

The NIHIL OBSTAT and IMPRIMATUR are a declaration that a book or pamphlet is considered to be free from doctrinal or moral error. It is not implied that those who have granted the NIHIL OBSTAT or IMPRIMATUR agree with the contents, opinions, or statements expressed.

Note to the reader: The full religious name of St. Faustina Kowalska was Sister Maria Faustina of the Most Blessed Sacrament. In the world, she was known as Helen Kowalska.

ISBN: 0-944203-41-8

Printed in the United States of America by the Marian Press

Table of Contents

Foreword

When the disciples saw Jesus praying, they were fascinated. They wanted to pray like Him. After He finished, they approached Him and asked: "Lord, teach us to pray" (Lk 11:1). Jesus responded by teaching them the prayer we know as the Our Father or the Lord's Prayer. But it was far more than an ordinary prayer, it was a statement of the very life of Jesus. The Our Father summarizes the mission of Jesus. His whole life was orientated to the glory of His Father. It was the Father's kingdom He proclaimed, the Father's will He came to do, the Father's mercy He made visible for us. As we pray the Our Father, we enter into the mission of Jesus to reveal the Father who is rich in mercy.

So, too, when we read the prayers recorded in the *Diary of Saint Faustina Kowalska,* we become fascinated. They express her mission as an apostle of Divine Mercy, and, as we pray with her, we enter into her spirit of trust in the mercy of God. How do we learn to pray? By actually praying. We learn from the masters. We learn from Jesus by repeating from the heart His prayer to the Father. We learn from Saint Faustina, whom Jesus called the apostle and secretary of The Divine Mercy. As we repeat the prayers she recorded in her *Diary*, we learn what made her so special. We learn how to become living witnesses of trust, relying on God's mercy in all the circumstances of our own lives. Saint Faustina was told by the Lord and by her spiritual director to write all that came to her mind (*Diary*, 1605) for the benefit of souls (895, 1142, 1317, 1471); and this included her spontaneous prayers. She wrote them freely from her heart with no indication that she ever re-read or corrected them.

The *Diary* is thus a treasure chest of prayers. A special selection of these prayers have been gathered together here and arranged to form a daily prayerbook for various times, moods, and needs. The prayers are grouped under general topics to help you in browsing through them. The numbers in parenthesis refer to paragraph numbers in the *Diary*. Do you want to grow as an apostle of Divine Mercy? Then pray these prayers of Saint Faustina, the apostle of Divine Mercy. Pray them frequently. Pray them from the heart.

Fr. George W. Kosicki, CSB

Note to the Reader

In addition to making Saint Faustina's prayers our own, we should also remember to include in our daily prayers the powerful prayers that Saint Faustina received from Jesus Himself. Among them are the Chaplet of Divine Mercy and the prayer of offering her sufferings:

O Blood and Water, which gushed forth from the Heart of Jesus as a Fount of Mercy for us, I trust in You (309).

These prayers are an essential part of the Divine Mercy message and devotion.

Throughout the text of this booklet, the reader should note that the numbers in parentheses correspond with the paragraph numbers found in the margins of the *Diary*. These parenthetical references signal to the reader that a particular prayer is finished. Further, wherever a new prayer starts, all of the letters of the first couple of words have been capitalized.

Introduction

As a college student, reading the *Diary* for the first time, I was profoundly moved by the depth and sincerity of Saint Faustina's spiritual life. It wasn't the revelations themselves that jumped out at me from those pages. It was, rather, Faustina's simple, honest prayers which expressed so clearly her intimate relationship with the Lord.

Her words inspired me to seek my own relationship with God, to turn my life over to Him, and to trust in His endless mercy. Her prayers were so real, so applicable to my own life, that I often found myself "borrowing" them as I spoke to God. How often, amid the craziness of college life, did I find myself praying:

> Jesus, my Master, guide me. Govern me according to Your will, purify my love that it may be worthy of You, do with me as Your most merciful Heart desires.
>
> ... Keep me, Jesus, in a recollected spirit! (218).

Now, with the increasing demands of being a wife and a mother, I have come to see that my sanity (not to mention my salvation) depends entirely on my ability to completely surrender to God's will, "which is Love and Mercy itself" (950). And no matter how busy I am, there is always time to say a little prayer to get myself back on track. My favorite these days is "King of Mercy, guide my soul" (3) — so simple, yet so perfect. The *Diary* is full of prayers like this.

But the prayers often get overlooked in the *Diary*, so for this booklet we have selected the ones which seem to be most universal. They are arranged in categories, to make it easier to pray for particular intentions or at particular times. Let us take advantage of these jewels of prayer given to us by this beautiful woman of God — who is the first saint of the new millennium!

Christ repeatedly tells us that if we are to enter the kingdom of Heaven, we must become like little children. As my son, Joseph, has so often demonstrated to me, to be childlike means to have *complete* trust. This is so difficult for most of us, and so I urge you, in the words of Saint Faustina, to "read these considerations on Divine Mercy and become trusting" (949).

Colleen Free

Short, Exclamatory Prayers
†

MOST Merciful Heart of Jesus, protect us from the just anger of God (1526).

O CHRIST, although much effort is required, all things can be done with Your grace (1696).

O MY JESUS, I am making at this very moment a firm and eternal resolution by virtue of Your grace and mercy, fidelity to the tiniest grace of Yours (716).

WITH JESUS, through Jesus and in Jesus is my communion with You, Eternal Father (648).

O MY GOD, I love You (1323).

KING OF MERCY, guide my soul (3).

JESUS, I trust in You; I trust in the ocean of Your mercy. You are a Mother to me (249).

O MY GOD, my only hope, I have placed all my trust in You, and I know I shall not be disappointed (317).

O PUREST LOVE, rule in all Your plenitude in my heart and help me to do Your holy will most faithfully! (328).

JESUS, Life and Truth, my Master, guide every step of my life, that I may act according to Your holy will (688).

MY JESUS, my strength and my only hope, in You alone is all my hope. My trust will not be frustrated (746).

O JESUS, have mercy! Embrace the whole world and press me to Your Heart ... O Lord, let my soul repose in the sea of Your unfathomable mercy (869).

HIDE ME, Jesus, in the depths of Your mercy, and then let my neighbor judge me as he pleases (791).

O JESUS, shield me with Your mercy and also judge me leniently, or else Your justice may rightly damn me (1093).

Transform Me into Yourself
†

O JESUS, continue to grant me Your divine life. Let Your pure and noble Blood throb with all its might in my heart. I give You my whole being. Transform me into Yourself and make me capable of doing Your holy will in all things and of returning Your love. ... May Your pure and omnipotent love be the driving force of all my actions. Who will ever conceive and understand the depth of mercy that has gushed forth from Your Heart? (832).

I EXPOSE my heart to the action of Your grace like a crystal exposed to the rays of the sun. May Your image be reflected in it, O my God, to the extent that it is possible to be reflected in the heart of a creature. Let Your divinity radiate through me, O You who dwell in my soul (1336).

MY JESUS, penetrate me through and through so that I might be able to reflect You in my whole life. Divinize me so that my deeds may have supernatural value. Grant that I may have love, compassion and mercy for every soul without exception. O my Jesus, each of Your saints reflects one of Your virtues; I desire to reflect Your compassionate heart, full of mercy; I want to glorify it. Let Your mercy, O Jesus, be impressed upon my heart and soul like a seal, and this will be my badge in this and the future life. Glorifying Your mercy is the exclusive task of my life (1242).

JESUS, make my heart like unto Yours, or rather transform it into Your own Heart that I may sense the needs of other hearts, especially those who are sad and suffering. May the rays of mercy rest in my heart (514).

JESUS, my Life, how well I feel that You are transforming me into Yourself, in the secrecy of my soul where the senses can no longer perceive much. O my Savior, conceal me completely in the depths of Your Heart and shield me with

Your rays against everything that is not You. I beg You, Jesus, let the two rays that have issued from Your most merciful Heart continuously nourish my soul (465).

I MUST be on my guard, especially today, because I am becoming over-sensitive to everything. Things I would not pay any attention to when I am healthy bother me today. ... O my Jesus, transform me into Yourself by the power of Your love, that I may be a worthy tool in proclaiming Your mercy (783).

Desire to Please God
†

O MY JESUS, Eternal Truth, I fear nothing, neither hardships nor sufferings; I fear only one thing, and that is to offend You. My Jesus, I would rather not exist than make You sad. Jesus, You know that my love knows no one but You. My soul is absorbed in You (571).

JESUS, I ask You with all my heart, let me know what there is in me that displeases You and also let me know what I should do to become more pleasing to You. Do not refuse me this favor and be with me. I know that without You, Lord, all my efforts will not amount to much. Oh, how I rejoice at Your greatness, O Lord! The more I come to know You, the more ardently I yearn for You and sigh after You! (273).

O MY JESUS, from the moment I gave myself completely to You, I have given no thought whatsoever for myself. You may do with me whatever You like. There is only one thing I think about; that is, what do You prefer; what can I do, O Lord, to please You. I listen and watch for each opportunity. It matters not if I am outwardly judged otherwise in this matter ... (1493).

Longing for God
†

OH, HOW GREAT is Your beauty, Jesus my Spouse! Living Flower enclosing life-giving dew for a thirsting soul! My soul is drowned in You. You alone are the object of my desires and strivings. Unite me as closely as possible to Yourself, to the Father and to the Holy Spirit. Let me live and die in You (501).

MY HEART is steeped in continual bitterness, because I want to go to You, Lord, into the fullness of life. O Jesus, what a dreadful wilderness this life seems to me! There is on this earth no nourishment for either my heart or my soul. I suffer because of my longing for You, O Lord. You have left me the Sacred Host, O Lord, but it enkindles in my soul an even greater longing for You, O my Creator and Eternal God! Jesus, I yearn to become united with You. Deign to hear the sighs of Your dearly beloved. Oh, how I suffer because I am still unable to be united with You. But let it be done according to Your wishes (867).

MY HEART wants nothing but You alone, O Treasure of my heart. For all the gifts You give me, thank you, O Lord, but I desire only Your Heart. Though the heavens are immense, they are nothing to me without You (969).

MY LOVE, reign in the most secret recesses of my heart, there where my most secret thoughts are conceived, where You alone have free access, in this deepest sanctuary where human thought cannot penetrate. May You alone dwell there, and may everything I do exteriorly take its origin in You. I ardently desire, and I am striving with all the strength of my soul, to make You, Lord, feel at home in this sanctuary (1721).

Love of God
†

O MY LORD, inflame my heart with love for You, that my spirit may not grow weary amidst the storms, the sufferings and the trials. You see how weak I am. Love can do all (94).

JESUS, King of Mercy, ... I beg You, by all the love with which Your Heart burns, to destroy completely within me my self-love and, on the other hand, to enkindle in my heart the fire of Your purest love (371).

O SUPREME GOOD, I want to love You as no one on earth has ever loved You before! I want to adore You with every moment of my life and unite my will closely to Your holy will. My life is not drab or monotonous, but it is varied like a garden of fragrant flowers, so that I don't know which flower to pick first, the lily of suffering or the rose of love of neighbor or the violet of humility. I will not enumerate these treasures in which my every day abounds. It is a great thing to know how to make use of the present moment (296).

ETERNAL LOVE, Depth of Mercy, O Triune Holiness, yet One God, whose bosom is full of love for all, as a good Father You scorn no one. O Love of God, Living Fountain, pour Yourself out upon us, Your unworthy creatures. May our misery not hold back the torrents of Your love, for indeed, there is no limit to Your mercy (1307).

O GREAT GOD, I admire Your goodness! You are the Lord of heavenly hosts, and yet You stoop so low to Your miserable creatures. Oh, how ardently I desire to love You with every beat of my heart! The whole extent of the earth is not enough for me, heaven is too small, and boundless space is nothing; You alone are enough for me, Eternal God! You alone can fill the depths of my soul (288).

O LOVE, O depth of Your abasement, O mystery of happiness, why do so few people know You? Why is Your love not returned? O Divine Love, why do You hide Your beauty?

O Infinite One beyond all understanding, the more I know You the less I comprehend You; but because I cannot comprehend You, I better comprehend Your greatness. I do not envy the Seraphim their fire, for I have a greater gift deposited in my heart. They admire You in rapture, but Your Blood mingles with mine. Love is heaven given us already here on earth. Oh, why do You hide in faith? Love tears away the veil. There is no veil before the eye of my soul, for You Yourself have drawn me into the bosom of secret love forever. Praise and glory be to You, O Indivisible Trinity, One God, unto ages of ages! (278).

> O JESUS, hidden God,
> My heart perceives You
> Though veils hide You;
> You know that I love You (524).

MY JESUS, delight of my heart, when my soul is filled with Your divinity, I accept sweetness and bitterness with the same equanimity. One and the other will pass away. All that I keep in my soul is the love of God. For this I strive; all else is secondary (1245).

> ALL THINGS will have an end
>   in this vale of tears,
> Tears will run dry and pain will cease.
> Only one thing will remain —
> Love for You, O Lord (1132).

Thanksgiving

†

THANK YOU, O God for all the graces
Which unceasingly You lavish upon me,
Graces which enlighten me with the
    brilliance of the sun,
For by them You show me the sure way.

Thank You, O Lord, for creating me,
For calling me into being from nothingness,
For imprinting Your divinity on my soul,
The work of sheer merciful love.

Thank You, O God, for Holy Baptism
Which engrafted me into Your family,
A gift great beyond all thought or expression
Which transforms my soul.

Thank You, O Lord, for Holy Confession,
For that inexhaustible spring of great mercy,
For that inconceivable fountain of graces
In which sin-tainted souls become purified.

Thank You, O Jesus, for Holy Communion
In which You give us Yourself.
I feel Your Heart beating within my breast
As You cause Your divine life to unfold
    within me.

Thank You, O Holy Spirit, for the
    Sacrament of Confirmation,
Which dubs me Your knight
And gives strength to my soul at each
    moment,
Protecting me from evil.

Thank You, O God, for the grace of
    a vocation
For being called to serve You alone,
Leading me to make You my sole love,
An unequal honor for my soul.

Thank You, O Lord, for perpetual vows,
For that union of pure love,
For having deigned to unite Your pure Heart
    with mine
And uniting my heart to Yours in the purest
    of bonds.

Thank You, O Lord, for the Sacrament of
    Anointing
Which, in my final moments, will give me
    strength;
My help in battle, my guide to salvation,
Fortifying my soul till we rejoice forever.

Thank You, O God, for all the inspirations
That Your goodness lavishes upon me,
For the interior lights given my soul,
Which the heart senses, but words cannot
    express.

Thank You, O Holy Trinity, for the vastness
of the graces
Which You have lavished on me unceasingly
through life.
My gratitude will intensify as the eternal
dawn rises,
When, for the first time, I sing to Your glory
(1286).

O JESUS, eternal God, thank You for Your
countless graces and blessings. Let every beat of
my heart be a new hymn of thanksgiving to You,
O God. Let every drop of my blood circulate for
You, Lord. My soul is one hymn in adoration of
Your mercy. I love You, God, for Yourself alone
(1794).

THANK YOU, O Lord, my Master,
That You have transformed me entirely into
Yourself,
And accompany me through life's toils and
labors;
I fear nothing when I have You in my heart
(1001).

YOU have surrounded my life with Your
tender and loving care, more than I can comprehend, for I will understand Your goodness in its
entirety only when the veil is lifted. I desire that
my whole life be but one act of thanksgiving to
You, O God (1285).

WELCOME to you, New Year, in the course of which my perfection will be accomplished. Thank You in advance, O Lord, for everything Your goodness will send me. Thank You for the cup of suffering from which I shall daily drink. Do not diminish its bitterness, O Lord, but strengthen my lips that, while drinking of this bitterness, they may know how to smile for love of You, my Master. I thank You for Your countless comforts and graces that flow down upon me each day like the morning dew, silently, imperceptibly, which no curious eye may notice, and which are know only to You and me, O Lord. For all this, I thank You as of today because, at the moment when You hand me the cup, my heart may not be capable of giving thanks (1449).

Offering of the Heart to Jesus
†

O MY MOST SWEET MASTER, good Jesus, I give You my heart. You shape and mold it after Your liking. O fathomless love, I open the calyx of my heart to You, like a rosebud to the freshness of dew. To You alone, my Betrothed, is known the fragrance of the flower of my heart. Let the fragrance of my sacrifice be pleasing to You. O Immortal God, my everlasting delight, already here on earth You are my heaven. May every beat of my heart be a new hymn of praise to You, O Holy Trinity! Had I as many hearts as there are drops of water in the ocean or grains of sand in the whole world, I would offer them all to You, O my Love, O Treasure of my heart! Whomever I shall meet in my life, no matter who they may be, I want to draw them all to love You, O my Jesus, my Beauty, my Repose, my sole Master, Judge, Savior, and Spouse, all in one; I know that one title will modify the other — I have entrusted everything to Your mercy (1064).

Eucharist, Jesus as Friend
†

O JESUS concealed in the Host, my sweet Master and faithful Friend, how happy my soul is to have such a Friend who always keeps me company. I do not feel lonely even though I am in isolation. Jesus-Host, we know each other — that is enough for me (877).

OH, HOW HAPPY I am to be a dwelling place for You, O Lord! My heart is a temple in which You dwell continually ... (1392).

I BOW DOWN before You, O Bread of
    Angels,
With deep faith, hope, and love
And from the depths of my soul I
 worship You,
Though I am but nothingness.

I bow down before You, O hidden God
And love You with all my heart.

21

The veils of mystery hinder me not at all;
I love You as do Your chosen ones in heaven.

I bow down before You, O Lamb of God
Who take away the sins of my soul,
Whom I receive into my heart each morn,
You who are my saving help (1324).

WELCOME, hidden Love, life of my soul! I welcome You, Jesus, under these insignificant forms of bread. Welcome, sweetest Mercy, who pour Yourself out for souls. Welcome, Infinite Goodness, who pour out everywhere torrents of Your graces. Welcome, O veiled Brightness, the Light of souls. Welcome, O Fount of inexhaustible mercy, O purest Spring from which life and holiness gush forth for us. Welcome, Delight of pure souls. Welcome, only Hope of sinful souls (1733).

O BLESSED HOST, in golden chalice
    enclosed for me,
That through the vast wilderness of exile
I may pass — pure, immaculate,
    undefiled;
Oh, grant that through the power of Your
    love this might come to be.

O Blessed Host, take up Your dwelling
    within my soul,
O Thou my heart's purest love!
With Your brilliance the darkness dispel.
Refuse not Your grace to a humble heart.

O Blessed Host, enchantment of all heaven,
Though Your beauty be veiled
And captured in a crumb of bread,
Strong faith tears away that veil (159)

O LIVING HOST, support me in this exile, that I may be empowered to walk faithfully in the footsteps of the Savior. I do not ask, Lord, that You take me down from the cross, but I implore You to give me the strength to remain steadfast upon it. I want to be stretched out upon the cross as You were, Jesus. I want all the tortures and pains that You suffered. I want to drink the cup of bitterness to the dregs (1484).

O JESUS, concealed in the Blessed Sacrament of the Altar, my only love and mercy, I commend to You all the needs of my body and soul. You can help me, because You are Mercy itself. In You lies all my hope (1751).

O LIVING HOST, my one and only strength, fountain of love and mercy, embrace the whole world, fortify faint souls. Oh, blessed be the instant and the moment when Jesus left us His most merciful Heart! (223).

O BLESSED HOST, in whom is contained the testament of God's mercy for us, and especially for poor sinners.

O Blessed Host, in whom is contained the Body and Blood of the Lord Jesus as proof of infinite mercy for us, and especially for poor sinners.

O Blessed Host, in whom is contained life eternal and of infinite mercy, dispensed in abundance to us and especially to poor sinners.

O Blessed Host, in whom is contained the mercy of the Father, the Son, and the Holy Spirit toward us, and especially toward poor sinners.

O Blessed Host, in whom is contained the infinite price of mercy which will compensate for all our debts, and especially those of poor sinners.

O Blessed Host, in whom is contained the fountain of living water which springs from infinite mercy for us, and especially for poor sinners.

O Blessed Host, in whom is contained the fire of purest love which blazes forth from the bosom of the Eternal Father, as from an abyss of infinite mercy for us, and especially for poor sinners.

O Blessed Host, in whom is contained the medicine for all our infirmities, flowing from infinite mercy, as from a fount, for us and especially for poor sinners.

O Blessed Host, in whom is contained the union between God and us through His infinite mercy for us, and especially for poor sinners.

O Blessed Host, in whom are contained all the sentiments of the most sweet Heart of Jesus toward us, and especially poor sinners.

O Blessed Host, our only hope in all the sufferings and adversities of life.

O Blessed Host, our only hope in the midst of darkness and of storms within and without.

O Blessed Host, our only hope in life and at the hour of our death.

O Blessed Host, our only hope in the midst of adversities and floods of despair.

O Blessed Host, our only hope in the midst of falsehood and treason.

O Blessed Host, our only hope in the midst of the darkness and godlessness which inundate the earth.

O Blessed Host, our only hope in the longing and pain in which no one will understand us.

O Blessed Host, our only hope in the toil and monotony of everyday life.

O Blessed Host, our only hope amid the ruin of our hopes and endeavors.

O Blessed Host, our only hope in the midst of the ravages of the enemy and the efforts of hell.

O Blessed Host, I trust in You when the burdens are beyond my strength and I find my efforts are fruitless.

O Blessed Host, I trust in You when storms toss my heart about and my fearful spirit tends to despair.

O Blessed Host, I trust in You when my heart is about to tremble and mortal sweat moistens my brow.

O Blessed Host, I trust in You when everything conspires against me and black despair creeps into my soul.

O Blessed Host, I trust in You when my eyes will begin to grow dim to all temporal things and, for the first time, my spirit will behold the unknown worlds.

O Blessed Host, I trust in You when my tasks will be beyond my strength and adversity will become my daily lot.

O Blessed Host, I trust in You when the practice of virtue will appear difficult for me and my nature will grow rebellious.

O Blessed Host, I trust in You when hostile blows will be aimed against me.

O Blessed Host, I trust in You when my toils and efforts will be misjudged by others.

O Blessed Host, I trust in You when Your judgements will resound over me; it is then that I will trust in the sea of Your mercy (356).

Hail to God's Mercy

†

HAIL, most merciful Heart of Jesus,
Living Fountain of all graces,
Our sole shelter, our only refuge;
In You I have the light of hope.

Hail, most compassionate Heart of my God,
Unfathomable living Fount of Love
From which gushes life for sinful man
And the Spring of all sweetness.

Hail, open Wound of the Most Sacred Heart,
From which the rays of mercy issued forth
And from which it was given us to draw life
With the vessel of trust alone.

Hail, God's goodness, incomprehensible,
Never to be measured or fathomed,
Full of love and mercy, though always holy,
Yet, like a good mother, ever bent o'er us.

Hail Throne of Mercy, Lamb of God,
Who gave Your life in sacrifice for me,
Before whom my soul humbles itself daily,
Living in faith profound (1321).

THE LOVE OF GOD is the flower — Mercy the fruit. Let the doubting soul read these considerations on Divine Mercy and become trusting:

Divine Mercy, gushing forth from the bosom of the Father, I trust in You

Divine Mercy, greatest attribute of God, I trust in You.

Divine Mercy, incomprehensible mystery, I trust in You.

Divine Mercy, fount gushing forth from the mystery of the Most Blessed Trinity, I trust in You.

Divine Mercy, unfathomed by any intellect, human or angelic, I trust in You.

Divine Mercy, from which wells forth all life and happiness, I trust in You.

Divine Mercy, better than the heavens, I trust in You.

Divine Mercy, source of miracles and wonders, I trust in You.

Divine Mercy, encompassing the whole universe, I trust in You.

Divine Mercy, descending to earth in the Person of the Incarnate Word, I trust in You.

Divine Mercy, which flowed out from the open wound of the Heart of Jesus, I trust in You.

Divine Mercy, enclosed in the Heart of Jesus for us, and especially for poor sinners, I trust in You.

Divine Mercy, unfathomed in the institution of the Sacred Host, I trust in You.

Divine Mercy, in the founding of Holy Church, I trust in You.

Divine Mercy, in the Sacrament of Holy Baptism, I trust in You.

Divine Mercy, in our justification through Jesus Christ, I trust in You.

Divine Mercy, accompanying us through our whole life, I trust in You.

Divine Mercy, embracing us especially at the hour of death, I trust in You.

Divine Mercy, endowing us with immortal life, I trust in You.

Divine Mercy, accompanying us every moment of our life, I trust in You.

Divine Mercy, shielding us from the fire of hell, I trust in You.

Divine Mercy, in the conversion of hardened sinners, I trust in You.

Divine Mercy, astonishment for Angels, incomprehensible to Saints, I trust in You.

Divine Mercy, unfathomed in all the mysteries of God, I trust in You.

Divine Mercy, lifting us out of every misery, I trust in You.

Divine Mercy, source of our happiness and joy, I trust in You.

Divine Mercy, in calling us forth from nothingness to existence, I trust in You.

Divine Mercy, embracing all the works of His hands, I trust in You.

Divine Mercy, crown of all of God's handiwork, I trust in You.

Divine Mercy, in which we are all immersed, I trust in You.

Divine Mercy, sweet relief for anguished hearts, I trust in You.

Divine Mercy, only hope of despairing souls, I trust in You.

Divine Mercy, repose of hearts, peace amidst fear, I trust in You.

Divine Mercy, delight and ecstasy of holy souls, I trust in You.

Divine Mercy, inspiring hope against all hope, I trust in You (949).

O MY JESUS, be patient with me. I will be more careful in the future. I will rely, not upon myself, but upon Your grace and Your very great goodness to miserable me (366).

GOD'S INFINITE GOODNESS IN CREATING MANKIND

GOD, who in Your mercy have deigned to call man from nothingness into being, generously have You bestowed upon him nature and grace. But that seemed too little for Your infinite goodness. In Your mercy, O Lord, You have given us everlasting life. You admit us to Your everlasting happiness and grant us to share in Your interior life. And You do this solely out of Your mercy. You bestow on us the gift of Your grace, only because You are good and full of love. You had no need of us at all to be happy, but You, O Lord, want to share Your own happiness with us. But man did not stand the test. You could have punished him, like the angels, with eternal rejection, but here Your mercy appeared, and the very depths of Your being were moved with great compassion, and You promised to restore our salvation. It is an incomprehensible abyss of Your compassion that You did not punish us as we deserved. May Your mercy be glorified, O Lord; we will praise it for endless ages. And the angels were amazed at the greatness of the mercy which You have shown for mankind ... (1743).

GOD'S INFINITE GOODNESS IN ADORNING THE WHOLE WORLD WITH BEAUTY IN ORDER TO MAKE MAN'S STAY ON EARTH PLEASANT.

O GOD, how generously Your mercy is spread everywhere, and You have done all this for man. Oh, how much You must love him, since Your love is so active on his behalf. O my Creator and Lord, I see on all sides the trace of Your hand and the seal of Your mercy, which embraces all created things. O my most compassionate Creator, I want to give You worship on behalf of all creatures and all inanimate creation; I call on the whole universe to glorify Your mercy. Oh, how great is Your goodness, O God! (1749).

GOD'S INFINITE GOODNESS IN REDEEMING MAN

GOD, You could have saved thousands of worlds with one word; a single sigh from Jesus would have satisfied Your justice. But You Yourself, Jesus, purely out of love for us, underwent such a terrible Passion. Your Father's justice would have been propitiated with a single sigh from You, and all Your self-abasement is solely the work of Your mercy and Your inconceivable love. On leaving the earth, O Lord, You wanted to stay with us, and so You left us Yourself in the Sacrament of the Altar, and You opened wide Your mercy to us. There is no misery that could exhaust You; You have called us all to this fountain of love, to this spring of God's compassion. Here is the tabernacle of Your mercy, here is the remedy for all our ills. To You, O living spring of mercy, all souls are drawn; some like deer, thirsting for Your love, others to wash the wound of their sins, and still others, exhausted by life, to draw strength. At the moment of Your death on the Cross, You bestowed upon us eternal life; allowing Your most holy side to be opened. You opened an inexhaustible spring of mercy for us, giving us Your dearest possession, the Blood and Water from Your Heart. Such is the omnipotence of Your mercy. From it all grace flows to us (1747).

To Be Merciful
†

O MOST HOLY TRINITY! As many times as I breathe, as many times as my heart beats, as many times as my blood pulsates through my body, so many thousand times do I want to glorify Your mercy.

I want to be completely transformed into Your mercy and to be Your living reflection, O Lord. May the greatest of all divine attributes, that of Your unfathomable mercy, pass through my heart and soul to my neighbor.

Help me, O Lord, that my eyes may be merciful, so that I may never suspect or judge from appearances, but look for what is beautiful in my neighbors' souls and come to their rescue.

Help me, that my ears may be merciful, so that I may give heed to my neighbors' needs and not be indifferent to their pains and moanings.

Help me, O Lord, that my tongue may be merciful, so that I should never speak negatively of my neighbor, but have a word of comfort and forgiveness for all.

Help me, O Lord, that my hands may be merciful and filled with good deeds, so that I may do only good to my neighbors and take upon myself the more difficult and toilsome tasks.

Help me, that my feet may be merciful, so that I may hurry to assist my neighbor, overcoming my own fatigue and weariness. My true rest is in the service of my neighbor.

Help me, O Lord, that my heart may be merciful so that I myself may feel all the sufferings of my neighbor. I will refuse my heart to no one. I will be sincere even with those who, I know, will abuse my kindness. And I will lock myself up in the most merciful Heart of Jesus. I will bear my own suffering in silence. May Your mercy, O Lord, rest upon me.

You Yourself command me to exercise the three degrees of mercy. The first: the act of mercy, of whatever kind. The second; the word of mercy — if I cannot carry out a work of mercy, I will assist by my words. The third: prayer — if I cannot show mercy by deeds or words, I can always do so by prayer. My prayer reaches out even there where I cannot reach out physically. O my Jesus, transform me into Yourself, for You can do all things (163).

O MY JESUS, teach me to open the bosom of mercy and love to everyone who asks for it. Jesus, my Commander, teach me so that all my prayers and deeds may bear the seal of Your mercy (755).

O JESUS, I understand that Your mercy is beyond all imagining, and therefore I ask You to make my heart so big that there will be room in it for the needs of all the souls living on the face of the earth. O Jesus, my love extends beyond the world, to the souls suffering in purgatory, and I want to exercise mercy toward them by means of indulgenced prayers. God's mercy is unfathomable and inexhaustible, just as God himself is unfathomable. Even if I were to use the strongest words there are to express this mercy of God, all this would be nothing in comparison with what it is in reality. O Jesus, make my heart sensitive to all the sufferings of my neighbor, whether of body or of soul. O my Jesus, I know that You act toward us as we act toward our neighbor.

My Jesus, make my heart like unto Your merciful Heart. Jesus, help me to go through life doing good to everyone (692).

O MERCIFUL JESUS, stretched on the cross, be mindful of the hour of our death. O most merciful Heart of Jesus, opened with a lance, shelter me at the last moment of my life. O Blood and Water, which gushed forth from the Heart of Jesus as a fount of unfathomable mercy for me at the hour of my death, O dying Jesus, Hostage of mercy, avert the Divine wrath at the hour of my death (813).

THANK YOU, JESUS, for the great favor of making known to me the whole abyss of my misery. I know that I am an abyss of nothingness and that, if Your holy grace did not hold me up, I would return to nothingness in a moment. And so, with every beat of my heart, I thank You, my God, for Your great mercy towards me (256).

DURING HOLY MASS, I offered myself completely to the heavenly Father through the sweetest Heart of Jesus; let Him do as He pleases with me. Of myself I am nothing, and in my misery I have nothing of worth; so I abandon myself into the ocean of Your mercy, O Lord (668).

O MY CREATOR and Lord, my entire being is Yours! Dispose of me according to Your divine pleasure and according to Your eternal plans and Your unfathomable mercy. May every soul know how good the Lord is; may no soul fear to commune intimately with the Lord; may no soul use unworthiness as an excuse, and may it never postpone [accepting] God's invitations, for that is not pleasing to the Lord. There is no soul more wretched than I am, as I truly know myself, and I am astounded that divine Majesty stoops so low. O eternity, it seems to me that you are too short to extol [adequately] the infinite mercy of the Lord! (440).

O GREATLY MERCIFUL GOD, Infinite Goodness, today all mankind calls out from the abyss of its misery to Your mercy — to Your compassion, O God; and it is with its mighty voice of misery that it cries out. Gracious God, do not reject the prayer of this earth's exiles! O Lord, Goodness beyond our understanding, who are acquainted with our misery through and through, and know that by our own power we cannot ascend to You, we implore You: anticipate us with Your grace and keep on increasing Your mercy in us, that we may faithfully do Your holy will all through our life and at death's hour. Let the omnipotence of Your mercy shield us from the darts of our salvation's enemies, that we may with confidence, as Your children, await Your final coming — that day know to You alone. And we expect to obtain everything promised us by Jesus in spite of all our wretchedness. For Jesus is our Hope: Through His merciful Heart, as through an open gate, we pass through to heaven (1570).

O MY JESUS, You are giving me back my health and life; give me also strength for battle, because I am unable to do anything without You. Give me strength, for You can do all things. You see that I am a frail child, and what can I do? I know the full power of Your mercy, and I trust that You will give me everything Your feeble child needs (898).

O merciful God, You do not despise us, but lavish Your graces on us continuously. You make us fit to enter Your kingdom, and in Your goodness You grant that human beings may fill the places vacated by the ungrateful angels. O God of great mercy, who turned Your sacred gaze away from the rebellious angels and turned it upon contrite man, praise and glory be to Your unfathomable mercy, O God who do not despise the lowly heart (1339).

You have conquered, O Lord, my stony heart with Your goodness. In trust and humility I approach the tribunal of Your mercy, where You Yourself absolve me by the hand of Your representative. O Lord, I feel Your grace and Your peace filling my poor soul. I feel overwhelmed by Your mercy, O Lord. You forgive me, which is more than I dared to hope for or could imagine. Your goodness surpasses all my desires. And now, filled with gratitude for so many graces, I invite You to my heart. I wandered. like a prodigal child gone astray; but you did not cease to be my Father. Increase Your mercy toward me, for You see how weak I am (1485).

JESUS, hide me in Your mercy and shield me against everything that might terrify my soul. Do not let my trust in Your mercy be disappointed. Shield me with the omnipotence of Your mercy, and judge me leniently as well (1480).

MY JESUS, support me when difficult and stormy days come, days of testing, days of ordeal, when suffering and fatigue begin to oppress my body and my soul. Sustain me, Jesus, and give me strength to bear suffering. Set a guard upon my lips that they may address no word of complaint to creatures. Your most merciful Heart is all my hope. I have nothing for my defense but only Your mercy; in it lies all my trust (1065).

O MY JESUS, in terrible bitterness and
    pain,
I yet feel the caress of Your Divine Heart.
Like a good mother, You press me to
    Your bosom,
And even now You give me to experience
    what the veil hides.

O my Jesus, in this wilderness and terror
    which surround me,
My heart still feels the warmth of Your
    gaze,

Which no storm can blot out from me,
As You give me the assurance of Your
    great love, O God.

O my Jesus, midst the great miseries of
   this life,
You shine like a star, O Jesus, protecting
   me from shipwreck.
And though my miseries be great,
I have great trust in the power of Your
   mercy.

O hidden Jesus, in the many struggles of
   my last hour,
May the omnipotence of Your grace be
   poured out upon my soul,
That at death's moment I may gaze upon
   You
And see You face to face, as do the
   chosen in heaven.

O my Jesus, midst the dangers which
   surround me,
I go through life with a cry of joy, my
   head raised proudly,
Because against Your Heart so filled with
   love, O Jesus,
All enemies will be crushed, all darkness
   dispelled (1479).

MERCIFUL JESUS, with You I go boldly and
courageously into conflicts and battles. In
Your Name, I will accomplish everything and
overcome everything. My God, Infinite Goodness,
I beg of You, let Your infinite mercy accompany
me always and in all things (859).

YOU EXPIRED, Jesus, but the source of life gushed forth for souls, and the ocean of mercy opened up for the whole world. O Fount of Life, unfathomable Divine Mercy, envelop the whole world and empty Yourself out upon us (1319).

ETERNAL GOD, in whom mercy is endless and the treasury of compassion inexhaustible, look kindly upon us and increase Your mercy in us, that in difficult moments we might not despair nor become despondent, but with great confidence submit ourselves to Your holy will, which is Love and Mercy itself (950).

Live in the Present Moment
†

O JESUS, I want to live in the present moment, to live as if this were the last day of my life. I want to use every moment scrupulously for the greater glory of God, to use every circumstance for the benefit of my soul. I want to look upon everything, from the point of view that nothing happens without the will of God. God of unfathomable mercy, embrace the whole world and pour Yourself out upon us through the merciful Heart of Jesus (1183).

Prayers for Enlightenment

†

O SWEET RAYS of God, enlighten me to the most secret depth, for I want to arrive at the greatest possible purity of heart and soul (852).

ETERNAL TRUTH, give me a ray of Your light that I may come to know You, O Lord, and worthily glorify Your infinite mercy. And at the same time, grant me to know myself, the whole abyss of misery that I am (727).

JESUS, give me an intellect, a great intellect, for this only, that I may understand You better; because the better I get to know You, the more ardently will I love You. Jesus, I ask You for a powerful intellect, that I may understand divine and lofty matters. Jesus, give me a keen intellect with which I will get to know Your Divine Essence and Your indwelling, Triune life. Give my intellect these capacities and aptitudes by means of Your special grace. Although I know that there is a capability through grace which the Church gives me, there is still a treasure of graces which You give us, O Lord, when we ask You for them. But if my request is not pleasing to You, then I beg You, do not give me the inclination to pray thus (1474).

O ETERNAL and incomprehensible Love, I beg You for one grace: enlighten my mind with light from on high; help me to know and appreciate all things according to their value. I feel the greatest joy in my soul when I come to know the truth (410).

Jesus, Our Defense and Guide
†

O JESUS, I am locking myself in Your most merciful Heart as in a fortress, impregnable against the missiles of my enemies (1535).

O MY JESUS, direct my mind, take possession of my whole being, enclose me in the depths of Your Heart, and protect me against the assaults of the enemy. My only hope is in You. Speak through my mouth when I, wretchedness itself, find myself with the mighty and wise, so that they will know that this undertaking is Yours and comes from You (76).

WITH THE TRUST and simplicity of a small child, I give myself to You today, O Lord Jesus, my Master. I leave You complete freedom in directing my soul. Guide me along the paths You wish. I won't question them. I will follow You trustingly. Your merciful Heart can do all things! (228).

JESUS, my Master, guide me. Govern me according to Your will, purify my love that it may be worthy of You, do with me as Your most merciful Heart desires ... Keep me, Jesus, in a recollected spirit! (218).

O MY JESUS, give me strength to endure suffering so that I may not make a wry face when I drink the cup of bitterness. Help me Yourself to make my sacrifice pleasing to You. May it not be tainted by my self-love, even though it extend over many years. May purity of intention make it pleasing to You, fresh and full of life. This life of mine is a ceaseless struggle, a constant effort to do Your holy will; but may everything that is in me, both my misery and my strength, give praise to You, O Lord (1740).

O JESUS, You know how weak I am; be then ever with me; guide my actions and my whole being, You who are my very best Teacher! Truly, Jesus, I become frightened when I look at my own misery, but at the same time I am reassured by Your unfathomable mercy, which exceeds my misery by the measure of all eternity. This disposition of soul clothes me in Your power. O joy that flows from the knowledge of one's self! O unchanging Truth, Your constancy is everlasting! (66)

MY JESUS, You see how weak I am of myself. Therefore, You Yourself direct my affairs. And know, Jesus, that without You I will not budge for any cause, but with You I will take on the most difficult things (602).

MY JESUS, despite Your graces, I see and feel all my misery. I begin my day with battle and end it with battle. As soon as I conquer one obstacle, ten more appear to take its place. But I am not worried, because I know that this is the time of struggle, not peace. When the burden of the battle becomes too much for me, I throw myself like a child into the arms of the heavenly Father and trust I will not perish. O my Jesus, how prone I am to evil, and this forces me to be constantly vigilant. But I do not lose heart, I trust God's grace, which abounds in the worst misery (606).

THE BARQUE of my life sails along
Amid darkness and shadows of night,
And I see no shore;
I am sailing the high seas.

The slightest storm would drown me,
Engulfing my boat in the swirling depths,
If You Yourself did not watch over me,
   O God,
At each instant and moment of my life.

Amid the roaring waves
I sail peacefully, trustingly,
And gaze like a child into the distance
   without fear,
Because You, O Jesus, are my Light.

Dread and terror is all about me,
But within my soul is peace more profound
   than the depths of the sea,
For he who is with You, O Lord, will not
   perish;
Of this Your love assures me, O God.

Though a host of dangers surround me,
None of them do I fear, for I fix my gaze on
    the starry sky,
And I sail along bravely and merrily,
As becomes a pure heart.

And if the ship of my life sails so peacefully,
This is due to but one thing above all:
You are my helmsman, O God.
This I confess with utmost humility (1322).

JESUS, Eternal Light, enlighten my mind,
strengthen my will, inflame my heart and be
with me as You have promised, for without You
I am nothing. You know, Jesus, how weak I am.
I do not need to tell You this, for You Yourself
know perfectly well how wretched I am. It is in
You that all my strength lies (495).

O TRUTH, O thorny life,
In order to pass through you victoriously
It is necessary to lean on You, O Christ,
And to be always close to You.

I would not know how to suffer without
    You, O Christ.
Of myself I would not be able to brave
    adversities.
Alone, I would not have the courage to
    drink from Your cup;
But You, Lord, are always with me, and
You lead me along mysterious paths.

A weak child, I have begun the battle in
   Your Name.
I have fought bravely, though often
   without success,
And I know that my efforts have pleased
   You,
And I know that it is the effort alone
   which You eternally reward.

O truth, O life-and-death struggle,
When I rose to do battle, an inexperi-
   enced knight,
I felt I had a knight's blood, though still a
   child,
And therefore, O Christ, I needed Your
   help and protection.

My heart will not rest from its efforts and
   struggle
Until You Yourself call me from the field
   of battle.
I will stand before You, not to receive a
   reward,
But to be drowned in You, in peace
   forever (1654).

WHEN PAIN overwhelms my soul,
And the horizon darkens like night,
And the heart is torn with the
   torment of suffering,
Jesus Crucified, You are my strength.

When the soul, dimmed with pain,
Exerts itself in battle without respite,
And the heart is in agony and torment,
Jesus Crucified, You are the hope of my
    salvation.

And so the days pass,
As the soul bathes in a sea of bitterness,
And the heart dissolves in tears,
Jesus Crucified, You shine for me like the
    dawn.

And when the cup of bitterness brims
    over,
And all things conspire against her,
And the soul goes down to the Garden of
    Olives,
Jesus Crucified, in You is my defense.

When the soul, conscious of its
    innocence,
Accepts these dispensations from God,
The heart can then repay hurts with love.
Jesus Crucified, transform my weakness
    into omnipotence (1151).

JESUS, Friend of a lonely heart, You are my
haven, You are my peace. You are my salvation,
You are my serenity in moments of struggle and
amidst an ocean of doubts. You are the bright
ray that lights up the path of my life. You are
everything to a lonely soul. You understand

the soul even though it remains silent. You know our weaknesses, and like a good physician, You comfort and heal, sparing us sufferings — expert that You are (247).

JESUS, my most perfect model, with my eyes fixed on You, I will go through life in Your footsteps, adapting nature to grace, according to Your most holy will and Your light which illumines my soul, trusting completely in Your help (1351).

HAIL TO YOU, Eternal Love, my Sweet Jesus, who have condescended to dwell in my heart! I salute You, O glorious Godhead who have deigned to stoop to me, and out of love for me have so emptied Yourself as to assume the insignificant form of bread. I salute You, Jesus, never-fading flower of humanity. You are all there is for my soul. Your love is purer than a lily, and Your presence is more pleasing to me than the fragrance of a hyacinth. Your friendship is more tender and subtle than the scent of a rose, and yet it is stronger than death. O Jesus, incomprehensible beauty, it is with pure souls that You communicate best, because they alone are capable of heroism and sacrifice. O sweet, rose-red blood of Jesus, ennoble my blood and change it into Your own blood, and let this be done to me according to Your good pleasure (1575).

Prayer for Healing
†

JESUS, may Your pure and healthy blood circulate in my ailing organism, and may Your pure and healthy body transform my weak body, and may a healthy and vigorous life throb within me, if it is truly Your holy will that I should set about the work in question; and this will be a clear sign of Your holy will for me (1089).

Trust in Suffering
†

O SUFFERING CHRIST, I am going out to meet You. As Your bride, I must resemble You. Your cloak of ignominy must cover me too. O Christ, You know how ardently I desire to become like You. Grant that Your entire Passion may be my lot. May all Your sorrow be poured into my heart. I trust that You will complete this in me in the way You deem most fitting (1418).

JESUS, who in the Gospel compare Yourself to a most tender mother, I trust in Your words because You are Truth and Life. In spite of every-thing, Jesus, I trust in You in the face of every interior sentiment which sets itself against hope. Do what You want with me; I will never leave You, because You are the source of my life (24).

O MY JESUS, nothing can lower my ideals, that is, the love which I have for You. Although the path is very thorny, I do not fear to go ahead. Even if a hailstorm of persecutions covers me; even if my friends forsake me; even if all things conspire against me, and the horizon grows dark; even if a raging storm breaks out, and I feel I am quite alone and must brave it all; still, fully at peace, I will trust in Your mercy, O my God, and my hope will not be disappointed (1195).

IN DIFFICULT and painful moments, O my Creator, I sing You a hymn of trust, for bottomless is the abyss of my trust in You and in Your mercy! (275).

O MY JESUS, despite the deep night that is all around me and the dark clouds which hide the horizon, I know that the sun never goes out. O Lord, though I cannot comprehend You and do not understand Your ways, I nonetheless trust in Your mercy. If it is Your will, Lord, that I live always in such darkness, may You be blessed. I ask You only one thing, Jesus: do not allow me to offend You in any way. O my Jesus, You alone know the longings and the sufferings of my heart. I am glad I can suffer for You, however little. When I feel that the suffering is more than I can bear, I take refuge in the Lord in the Blessed Sacrament, and I speak to Him with profound silence (73).

O JESUS, eternal Truth, strengthen my feeble forces; You can do all things, Lord. I know that without You all my efforts are in vain. O Jesus, do not hide from me, for I cannot live without You. Listen to the cry of my soul. Your mercy has not been exhausted, Lord, so have pity on my misery. Your mercy surpasses the understanding of all Angels and people put together; and so, although it seems to me that You do not hear me, I put my trust in the ocean of Your mercy, and I know that my hope will not be deceived (69).

MY TORMENTED soul finds aid nowhere but in You, O Living Host. I place all my trust in Your merciful Heart. I am waiting patiently for Your word, Lord (1138).

JESUS, do not leave me alone in suffering. You know, Lord, how weak I am. I am an abyss of wretchedness, I am nothingness itself; so what will be so strange if You leave me alone and I fall? I am an infant, Lord, so I cannot get along by myself. However, beyond all abandonment I trust, and in spite of my own feeling I trust, and I am being completely transformed into trust — often in spite of what I feel. Do not lessen any of my sufferings, only give me strength to bear them. Do with me as You please, Lord, only give me the grace to be able to love You in every event and circumstance. Lord, do not lessen my cup of bitterness, only give me strength that I may be able to drink it all.

O Lord, sometimes You lift me up to the brightness of visions, and then again You plunge me into the darkness of night and the abyss of my nothingness, and my soul feels as if it were alone in the wilderness. Yet, above all things, I trust in You, Jesus, for You are unchangeable. My moods change, but You are always the same, full of mercy (1489).

Suffering in the Present Moment
†

O MY GOD, how sweet it is to suffer for You, suffer in the most secret recesses of the heart, in the greatest hiddenness, to burn like a sacrifice noticed by no one, pure as crystal, with no consolation or compassion. My spirit burns in active love. I waste no time in dreaming. I take every moment singly as it comes, for this is within my power. The past does not belong to me; the future is not mine; with all my soul I try to make use of the present moment (351).

Offering Suffering
†

O SAVIOR of the world, I unite myself with Your mercy. My Jesus, I join all my sufferings to Yours and deposit them in the treasury of the Church for the benefit of souls (740).

O Christ, may delights, honor, and glory be Yours, and suffering be mine. I will not lag one step behind as I follow You, though thorns wound my feet (70).

O Christ, suffering for You is the delight of my heart and my soul. Prolong my sufferings to infinity, that I may give You a proof of my love. I accept everything that Your hand will hold out to me. Your love, Jesus, is enough for me. I will glorify You in abandonment and darkness, in agony and fear, in pain and bitterness, in anguish of spirit and grief of heart. In all things may You be blessed. My heart is so detached from the earth, that You Yourself are enough for me. There is no longer any moment in my life for self concern (1662).

My God, although my sufferings are great and protracted, I accept them from Your hands as magnificent gifts. I accept them all, even the ones that other souls have refused to accept. You can come to me with everything, my Jesus; I will refuse You nothing. I ask You for only one thing: give me the strength to endure them and grant that they may be meritorious. Here is my whole being; do with me as You please (1795).

O my Jesus, my soul was yearning for the days of trial, but do not leave me alone in the darkness of my soul. Rather, do You hold me firmly, close to Yourself. Set a guard over my lips, so that the fragrance of my sufferings may be known and pleasing to You alone (831).

TRUE LOVE is measured by the thermometer of suffering. Jesus, I thank You for the little daily crosses, for opposition to my endeavors, for the hardships of communal life, for the misinterpretation of my intentions, for humiliations at the hands of others, for the harsh way in which we are treated, for false suspicions, for poor health and loss of strength, for self-denial, for dying to myself, for lack of recognition in everything, for the upsetting of all my plans.

Thank You, Jesus, for interior sufferings, for dryness of spirit, for terrors, fears and incertitudes, for the darkness and the deep interior night, for temptations and various ordeals, for torments too difficult to describe, especially for those which no one will understand, for the hour of death with its fierce struggle and all its bitterness.

I thank You, Jesus, You who first drank the cup of bitterness before You gave it to me, in a much milder form. I put my lips to this cup of Your holy will. Let all be done according to Your good pleasure; let that which Your wisdom ordained before the ages be done to me. I want to drink the cup to its last drop, and not seek to know the reason why. In bitterness is my joy, in hopelessness is my trust. In You, O Lord, all is good, all is a gift of Your paternal Heart. I do not prefer consolations over bitterness or bitterness over consolations, but thank You, O Jesus, for everything! It is my delight to fix my gaze upon

You, O incomprehensible God! My spirit abides in these mysterious dwelling places, and there I am at home. I know very well the dwelling place of my Spouse. I feel there is not a single drop of blood in me that does not burn with love for You.

O Uncreated Beauty, whoever comes to know You once cannot love anything else. I can feel the bottomless abyss of my soul, and nothing will fill it but God Himself. I feel that I am drowned in Him like a single grain of sand in a bottomless ocean (343).

Sacrifice

MY JESUS, let my sacrifice burn before Your throne in all silence, but with the full force of love, as I beg You to have mercy on souls (1342).

O JESUS, I long for the salvation of immortal souls. It is in sacrifice that my heart will find free expression, in sacrifice which no one will suspect. I will burn and be consumed unseen in the holy flames of the love of God. The presence of God will help my sacrifice to be perfect and pure (235).

TODAY I place my heart on the paten where Your Heart has been placed, O Jesus, and today I offer myself together with You to God, Your

Father and mine, as a sacrifice of love and praise. Father of Mercy, look upon the sacrifice of my heart, but through the wound in the Heart of Jesus.

Jesus, I trust in You! Jesus, I love You with all my heart! When times are most difficult, You are my Mother.

For love of You, O Jesus, I die completely to myself today and begin to live for the greater glory of Your Holy Name.

Love, it is for love of You, O Most Holy Trinity, that I offer myself to You as an oblation of praise, as a holocaust of total self-immolation. And through this self-immolation, I desire the exaltation of Your Name, O Lord. I cast myself as a little rosebud at Your feet, O Lord, and may the fragrance of this flower be know to You alone (239).

Acceptance of God's Will
†

MAY YOU be blessed, O God, for everything You send me. Nothing under the sun happens without Your will. I cannot penetrate Your secrets with regard to myself, but I press my lips to the chalice You offer me (1208).

O JESUS, what darkness is enveloping me and what nothingness is penetrating me. But, my Jesus, do not leave me alone; grant me the grace of faithfulness. Although I cannot penetrate the mystery of God's visitation, it is in my power to say: Your will be done (1237).

O MY GOD, I am ready to accept Your will in every detail, whatever it may be. However You may direct me, I will bless You. Whatever You ask of me I will do with the help of Your grace. Whatever Your holy will regarding me might be, I accept it with my whole heart and soul, taking no account of what my corrupt nature tells me (1356).

DO WHAT YOU WILL with me, O Jesus; I will adore You in everything. May Your will be done in me, O my Lord and my God, and I will praise Your infinite mercy (78).

I AM TOTALLY in accord with Your will; do with me as You please, O Lord, but only grant me the grace of loving You more and more ardently. This is what is most precious to me. I desire nothing but You, O Love Eternal! It matters not along what paths You will lead me, paths of pain or paths of joy. I want to love You at every moment of my life (751).

ETERNAL GOD, Goodness itself, whose mercy is incomprehensible to every intellect, whether human or angelic, help me your feeble child, to do Your holy will as You make it known to me. I desire nothing but to fulfill God's desires. Lord, here are my soul and my body, my mind and my will, my heart and all my love. Rule me according to Your eternal plans (492).

So TODAY I submit myself completely and with loving consent to Your holy will, O Lord, and to Your most wise decrees, which are always full of clemency and mercy for me, though at times I can neither understand nor fathom them. O my Master, I surrender myself completely to You, who are the rudder of my soul; steer it Yourself according to Your divine wishes. I enclose myself in Your most compassionate Heart, which is a sea of unfathomable mercy (1450).

O LIGHT ETERNAL, who came to this earth, enlighten my mind and strengthen my will that I may not give up in times of great affliction. May Your light dissipate all the shadows of doubt. May Your omnipotence act through me. I trust in You, O uncreated Light! You, O Infant Jesus, are a model for me in accomplishing Your Father's will, You, who said, "Behold, I come to do Your will." Grant that I also may do God's will faithfully in all things. O Divine Infant, grant me this grace! (830)

O ETERNAL LOVE, who enkindles a new life within me, a life of love and of mercy, support me with Your grace, so that I may worthily answer Your call, so that what You Yourself have intended to accomplish in souls through me, might indeed be accomplished (1365).

O JESUS, stretched out upon the cross, I implore You, give me the grace of doing faithfully the most holy will of Your Father, in all things, always and everywhere. And when this will of God will seem to me very harsh and difficult to fulfill, it is then I beg You, Jesus, may power and strength flow upon me from Your wounds, and may my lips keep repeating, "Your will be done, O Lord." O Savior of the world, Lover of man's salvation who in such terrible torment and pain forget Yourself to think only of the salvation of souls, O most compassionate Jesus, grant me the grace to forget myself that I may live totally for souls, helping You in the work of salvation, according to the most holy will of Your Father ... (1265).

God's Greatness and My Wretchedness
†

O MY LORD, my soul is the most wretched of all, and yet You stoop to it with such kindness! I see clearly Your greatness and my littleness, and therefore I rejoice that You are so powerful and without limit, and so I rejoice greatly at being so little (1417).

Mary, Mother of God and Our Mother

†

O MARY, Immaculate Virgin,
Pure crystal for my heart,
You are my strength, O sturdy anchor!
You are the weak heart's shield and
   protection.

O Mary, you are pure, of purity
   incomparable;
At once both Virgin and Mother,
You are beautiful as the sun, without
   blemish,
And your soul is beyond all comparison.

Your beauty has delighted the eye of the
   Thrice-Holy One.
He descended from heaven, leaving His
   eternal throne,
And took Body and Blood of your heart
And for nine months lay hidden in a
   Virgin's heart.

O Mother, Virgin, purest of all lilies,
Your heart was Jesus' first tabernacle on
   earth.
Only because no humility was deeper
   than yours
Were you raised above the choirs of
   Angels and above all Saints.

O Mary, my sweet Mother,
I give you my soul, my body, and my
 poor heart.
Be the guardian of my life,
Especially at the hour of death, in the
 final strife (161).

> O SWEET MOTHER of God,
> I model my life on you;
> You are for me the bright dawn;
> In you I lose myself, enraptured.
>
> O Mother, Immaculate Virgin,
> In you the divine ray is reflected,
> Midst storms, 'tis you who teach
> me to love the Lord,
> O my shield and defense from the
> foe (1232).

O MARY, my Mother and my Lady, I offer
you my soul, my body, my life, and my death,
all that will follow it. I place everything in your
hands. O my Mother, cover my soul with your
virginal mantle and grant me the grace of purity
of heart, soul, and body. Defend me with your
power against all enemies, and especially
against those who hide their malice behind the
mask of virtue. O lovely lily! You are for me a
mirror, O my Mother! (79)

O RADIANT VIRGIN, pure as crystal, all
immersed in God, I offer you my spiritual life;
arrange everything that it may be pleasing to your
Son (844).

MARY, Immaculate Virgin, take me under your special protection and guard the purity of my soul, heart, and body. You are the model and star of my life (874).

O VIRGIN most pure, but also most humble, help me to attain deep humility (1306).

MOTHER OF GOD, your soul was plunged into a sea of bitterness; look upon your child and teach her to suffer and to love while suffering. Fortify my soul that pain will not break it. Mother of grace, teach me to live by [the power of] God (315).

O MARY, my Mother, I humbly beg of you, cover my soul with your virginal cloak at this very important moment of my life, so that thus I may become dearer to your Son and may worthily praise your Son's mercy before the whole world and throughout all eternity (220).

O MARY, today a terrible sword has pierced your holy soul. Except for God, no one knows of your suffering. Your soul does not break; it is brave, because it is with Jesus. Sweet Mother, unite my soul to Jesus, because it is only then that I will be able to endure all trials and tribulations, and only in union with Jesus will my little sacrifices be pleasing to God. Sweetest Mother, continue to teach me about the interior life. May the sword of suffering never break me. O pure Virgin, pour courage into my heart and guard it (915).

Parent and Child
†

CHRIST AND LORD, You are leading me over such precipices that, when I look at them, I am filled with fright, but at the same time I am at peace as I nestle close to Your heart. Close to Your Heart, I fear nothing. In these dangerous moments, I act like a little child, carried in its mother's arms; when it sees something which menaces it, it clasps its mother's neck more firmly and feels secure (1726).

O GOD, how much I desire to be a small child. You are my Father, and You know how little and weak I am. So I beg You, keep me close by Your side all my life and especially at the hour of my death, Jesus, I know that Your goodness surpasses the goodness of a most tender mother (242).

O MY JESUS, keep me near to You! See how weak I am! I cannot go a step forward by myself; so You, Jesus, must stand by me constantly like a mother by a helpless child — and even more so (264).

JESUS, living Host, You are my Mother, You are my all! It is with simplicity and love, with faith and trust that I will always come to You, O

Jesus! I will share everything with You, as a child with its loving mother, my joys and sorrows — in a word, everything (230).

O MY JESUS, the Life, the Way and the Truth, I beg You to keep me close to You as a mother holds a baby to her bosom, for I am not only a helpless child, but an accumulation of misery and nothingness (298).

The Holy Trinity
†

O HOLY TRINITY, in whom is contained the inner life of God, the Father, the Son, and the Holy Spirit, eternal joy, inconceivable depth of love, poured out upon all creatures and constituting their happiness, honor and glory be to Your holy Name forever and ever. Amen (525).

O HOLY TRINITY, Eternal God, my spirit is drowned in Your beauty. The ages are as nothing in Your sight. You are always the same. Oh, how great is Your majesty (576).

O HOLY TRINITY, Eternal God, I want to shine in the crown of Your mercy as a tiny gem whose beauty depends on the ray of Your light and of Your inscrutable mercy. All that is beautiful in my soul is Yours, O God; of myself, I am ever nothing (617).

Prayer to the Divine Spirit

✝

O DIVINE SPIRIT, Spirit of truth and of
    light,
Dwell ever in my soul by Your divine
    grace.
May Your breath dissipate the darkness,
And in this light may good deeds be
    multiplied.

O Divine Spirit, Spirit of love and of
    mercy,
Who pour the balm of trust into my heart,
Your grace confirms my soul in good,
Giving it the invincible power of
    constancy.

O Divine Spirit, Spirit of peace and of
    joy,
You invigorate my thirsting heart
And pour into it the living fountain of
    God's love,
Making it intrepid for battle.

O Divine Spirit, my soul's most welcome
    guest,
For my part, I want to remain faithful to
    You;

Both in days of joy and in the agony of
  suffering,
I want always, O Spirit of God, to live in
  Your presence.

O Divine Spirit, who pervade my whole
  being
And give me to know Your Divine
  Threefold Life,
Initiating me into Your Divine Essence,
Thus united to You, I will live a life
  without end (1411).

Prayer for Priests
†

O MY JESUS, I beg You on behalf of the
whole Church; Grant it love and the light of
Your Spirit, and give power to the words of
priests so that hardened hearts might be brought
to repentance and return to You, O Lord. Lord,
give us holy priests; You yourself maintain them
in holiness. O Divine and Great High Priest,
may the power of Your mercy accompany them
everywhere and protect them from the devil's
traps and snares which are continually being set
for the souls of priests. May the power of Your
mercy, O Lord, shatter and bring to naught all
that might tarnish the sanctity of priests, for You
can do all things (1052).

Prayer for One's Native Country

†

MOST MERCIFUL JESUS, I beseech You through the intercession of Your Saints, and especially the intercession of Your dearest Mother who nurtured You from childhood, bless my native land. I beg You, Jesus, look not on our sins, but on the tears of little children, on the hunger and cold they suffer. Jesus, for the sake of these innocent ones, grant me the grace that I am asking of You for my country (286).

Night Prayer

†

GOOD NIGHT, my Jesus; the bell is calling me to sleep. My Jesus, You see that I am dying from the desire to save souls. Good night, my Beloved; I rejoice at being one day closer to eternity. And if You let me wake up tomorrow, Jesus, I shall begin a new hymn to Your praise (679)

Prayer Intentions

Prayer Intentions

Prayer Intentions

Booklets on
Divine Mercy

The Divine Mercy Message and Devotion
by Fr. Seraphim Michalenko, MIC, and Vinny Flynn

This immensely popular booklet provides you with a complete introduction to the Divine Mercy message and devotion. Comes with plastic cover. 89 pages. **M17 ....$3.00**

Come to My Mercy
by Fr. George W. Kosicki, CSB

A complete step-by-step instruction manual for how to give and receive mercy. Here are the promises and desires of the Merciful Savior as recorded in the *Diary of Saint Faustina*. Comes with plastic cover. 32 pages. **DML12 ......$2.50**

Conversations with the Merciful God
by Fr. George W. Kosicki, CSB, and Vinny Flynn

Moving conversations between the Merciful Savior and five kinds of souls: sinful, despairing, suffering, striving, and perfect. All taken from the *Diary of Saint Faustina*. Comes with plastic cover. 32 pages. **BKC..........$2.50**